the Adjacent

Creator and Writer
PETER ZAHOS

Co-Writer
KRISTOPHER WHITE

Pencils/Inks:
RAY-ANTHONY HEIGHT, Chapter 1
MIGUEL ANGEL RUIZ GARRIDO, Chapter 2
JOSH ADAMS, Chapter 3 (6 pages)
TONE RODRIGUEZ, Chapter 3 (2 pages), Chapter 4
ATHILA FABBIO, Chapter 5 - 8

Colors: THOMAS CHU
Letters: ANDWORLD DESIGN
Cover: STEPHANE ROUX
Title Design: BRANDON DeSTEFANO
Concept Art: JOHN HOLMES

Special thanks to: Marcelo Ferreira de Almeida, Kate Powers, Michael Gerber, Saori Tsujimoto, Erica Carlson-Schultz, Stephen Christy, Chris Spellman, Neal Adams and Lia Ilgen

Chapter 1

DO YOU EVER LOOK AT THE WORLD AROUND YOU AND THINK THAT IT ALL LOOKS *WRONG?*
NIEUW ORANGE CELEBRATES 350TH ANNIVERSARY!
How Captain Colve Changed the World in 1673.
NOTHING IS FAMILIAR. NOT EVEN YOUR OWN REFLECTION.
JANE, YOU OKAY?
YEAH. I'M JUST NERVOUS. WE'VE NEVER BEEN SO CLOSE TO FINDING OUT WHERE I CAME FROM.
THE CONDITIONS MATCH THOSE THAT PRECIPITATED YOUR MIRACULOUS "ARRIVAL," YES. BUT THAT DOESN'T MEAN WE'RE GOING TO GET **ANSWERS.**
JUST MORE QUESTIONS.
YOU KNOW, FOR A *THREE YEAR OLD*, YOU HAVE A LOT OF ANXIETY, MS. HINDE.
EDUARDO, PLEASE. I *HATE* THAT NAME. IT MAKES ME FEEL... LOST. UNCLAIMED.
PSYCHOLOGISTS CALL IT *DISSOCIATION* - LITERALLY A BREAK FROM REALITY IN YOUR HEAD.

NIEUW ORANGE, 2023
BUT WHAT DO YOU CALL IT IF IT'S NOT IN YOUR HEAD?
the Adjacent
Written and Created by Peter Zahos

HEY, WE GAVE YOU A CHANCE TO CHOOSE A NEW NAME. YOU STUCK WITH IT.

YOU'D BEEN CALLING ME JANE FOR THREE YEARS. IT WASN'T REALLY A CHOICE.
SPACE TOREN
FL 298
WHAT CAN I SAY? IT'S BETTER THAN "SHE-WHO-APPEARS-IN-FIRE-BALLS."
...WHICH EXPLAINS YOUR RED HAIR.

C'MON. THE BOSON SURGE WAS DETECTED ON THE 118TH FLOOR. WE'LL TAKE THE LIFT FROM HERE.
AND REMEMBER, FOLLOW MY ORDERS. I HAD TO FIGHT COMMAND TO LET YOU IN THE FIELD.

I GUESS IT DEPENDS ON WHAT KIND OF ORDERS YOU GIVE ME.

WHAT'S THAT SUPPOSED TO MEAN?
YOU FIGURE IT OUT...

AFTER ALL, I AM A RED HEAD.
THOOOM

TACHYON LEVELS ARE THROUGH THE ROOF AND RISING! THIS WHOLE AREA IS UNSTABLE.
SO MUCH FOR EXACT CONDITIONS.
I'M CALLING IN THE REST OF THE PROTECTORAAT. NO TELLING WHAT WE'RE DEALING WITH.
WHAT... THE...HELL... IS...THAT?
I DON'T KNOW, BUT I THINK IT'S GOING TO--
CHOOOOM

EDUARDO!
HOLD ON!
YOU OKAY?
YEAH. LET'S JUST FIGURE OUT WHAT THAT ENERGY SPIKE WAS.
ACTUALLY. I THINK THAT'S GOING TO HAVE TO WAIT...
OH CRAP.

EDUARDO, GIVE ME ONE OF YOUR GUNS! THERE'S TOO MANY OF THEM!
NO! JUST GET BEHIND ME.

SWAPP

JANE! RUN!

SCREEEEEEEL
GET AWAY FROM HER!!

WHAT THE HELL...
COMMAND, WE HAVE A SITUATION!

LOOK OUT!

WHAT THE HELL? ARE YOU NAKED?!
MOST PEOPLE WOULD SAY THANKS.
SORRY ABOUT THOSE CREATURES. I THOUGHT I LOST THEM WHEN I TRANSVERSED SUPERSTRINGS.
ARE YOU SAYING YOU CAME FROM A DIFFERENT WORLD?
YOU MEAN... YOU DON'T RECOGNIZE ME?
I'M NICHOLAS ZACHARIAS... YOUR HUSBAND.
BUT I GUESS THAT'LL HAVE TO WAIT.

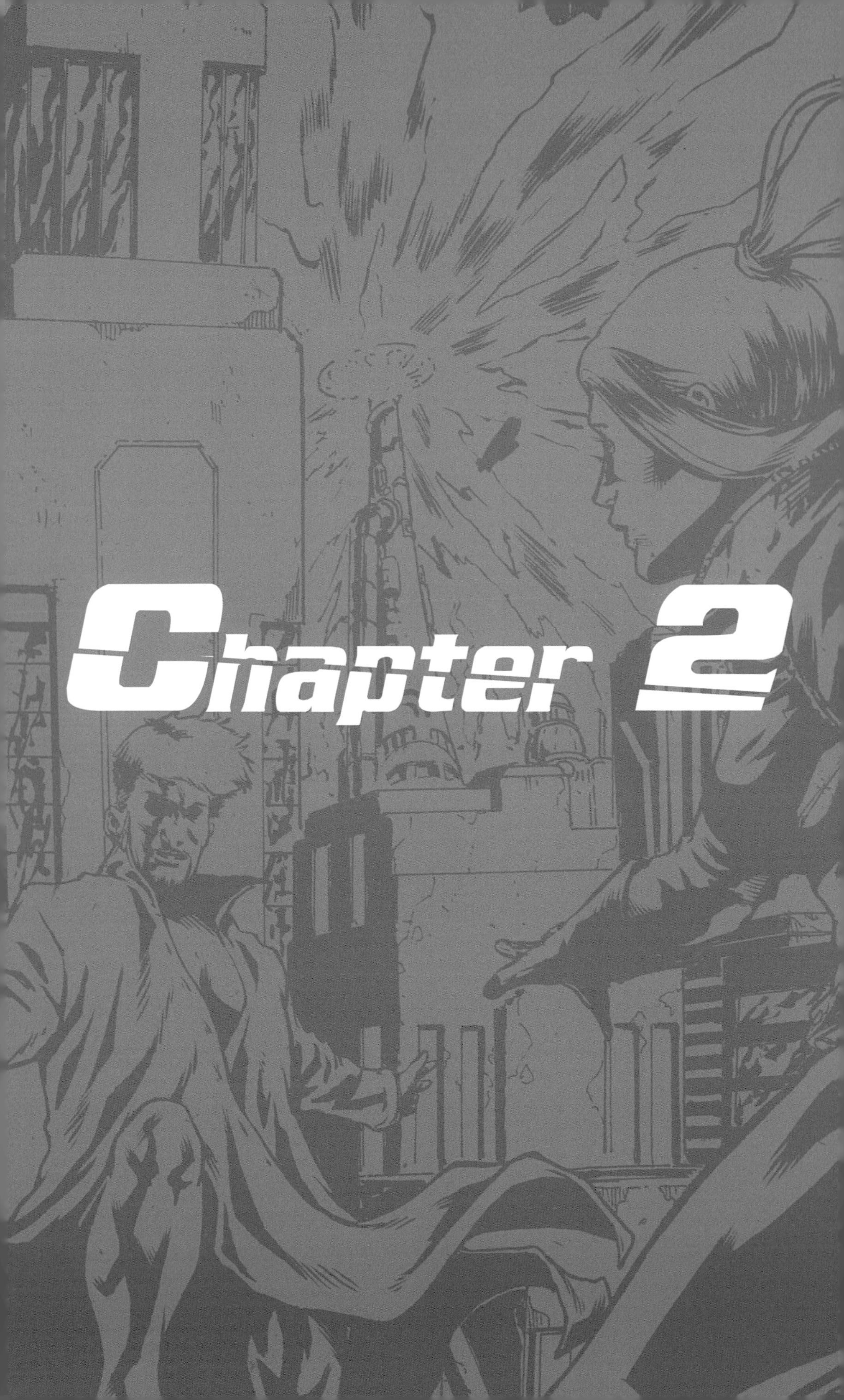
Chapter 2

SCREEEEEEEEE
HOLD MY HAND...THIS IS GOING TO FEEL WEIRD.
FOOM
WHAT DID YOU--DID YOU STOP TIME?
THAT'LL SLOW THEM DOWN. C'MON!

THE JUMPING GAVE ME EXTRA TEMPORAL ENERGY. YOU CAN DO THE SAME THING, PROBABLY MORE SO SINCE YOU'VE BEEN HERE LONGER.

WAIT A SECOND. I'M NOT GOING ANYWHERE WITH YOU.
JUST BECAUSE YOU *SAID* YOU'RE MY HUSBAND DOESN'T MEAN IT'S TRUE.
IN FACT, ALL OF THIS... IT'S A LITTLE FANTASTICAL.
IT'S BECAUSE I'M HALF-NAKED, ISN'T IT?

LOOK, I KNOW THIS WHOLE THING IS HARD TO ACCEPT-- ESPECIALLY IF YOU DON'T REMEMBER ME.
BUT TRUST ME WHEN I SAY, I'M HERE TO RESCUE YOU AND BRING YOU BACK TO OUR COMPOSITION. OUR *HOME.*

WHAT WERE THOSE THINGS? YOU SAID THEY FOLLOWED YOU?

VERSLINDER. THAT'S WHAT THEY CALL THEM. THEY'RE LIKE TERMITES, EXCEPT ON A QUANTUM LEVEL.
IN OTHER WORDS, THEY *DEVOUR* SPACE AND TIME... WHICH JUST MAKES THEM MULTIPLY FASTER.
NO. THIS IS... PHYSICAL TRANSFER BETWEEN N-DIMENSIONAL SPACE IS IMPOSSIBLE. I'VE STUDIED IT.

I SAID THE SAME THING. UNTIL *YOU* INVENTED A WAY TO DO IT.

JANE, CAN YOU HEAR ME? WE'RE GOING TO GET YOU OUT OF THERE. ARE YOU SAFE?
I CAN HEAR YOU!
PSFFFFFFTTTT

JANE, EH? THAT'S SUCH A PLAIN NAME. TO ME YOU'LL ALWAYS BE ALEXA.
ALEXA?

LOOK, THE VERSLINDER WILL BE BACK, I NEED TO GET YOU OUT OF HERE. THESE PEOPLE CAN'T HELP YOU.

THEY'VE HELPED ME FOR THE LAST THREE YEARS. YOU HAVEN'T.
SO I KINDLY DISAGREE.

YOU DON'T SEE IT! ALL THEY'VE DONE IS LIE TO YOU!
BUT I CAN SEE YOU'RE GOING TO HAVE TO DISCOVER THAT ON YOUR OWN!

ASK THEM ABOUT THE DEVICE THAT BROUGHT YOU HERE!
WHEN THEY FOUND ME, I HAD NOTHING ON ME. NO DEVICE. NO NOTHING.
AND IF THAT'S THE CASE, WHERE'S YOUR DEVICE?

IT'S GONE. DESTROYED.
THE ONE I HAD WAS JUST A PALE IMITATION OF YOURS. AN EARLY PROTOTYPE, IF YOU WILL.

WHICH MEANS YOUR DEVICE IS THE KEY TO GETTING US HOME.
PSFFFFFFFF
AND IF IT'S GONE?

THEN YOU'LL HAVE TO REBUILD IT.
BUT I CAN'T! I DON'T REMEMBER ANYTHING!

WELL, WHEN YOU'RE READY... WE CAN FIX THAT TOO.

CAREFUL...

I GOT YOU, JANE.

WHAT THE HELL WERE THOSE THINGS?
DON'T KNOW. FIRST TIME I'D EVER SEEN THEM IN MY LIFE. THEY WERE CREEPY THOUGH, THAT'S FOR SURE.
WE CALL THEM *VERSLINDER*...

MEANS DEVOURER. I CAME UP WITH THAT ONE.
COMMANDER COOLEN. WHAT ARE YOU DOING HERE?
WHAT DO YOU THINK? YOU CALLED FOR BACKUP. WHO'D YOU EXPECT? THE SECRETARY?
NOW, TELL ME... WHO THE HELL WAS THAT MAN?

I DON'T KNOW. HE SAID... HE SAID HE WAS MY **HUSBAND.** THAT WE BOTH CAME FROM ANOTHER PLANE OF EXISTENCE... ANOTHER **COMPOSITION.**

WHAT ELSE DID HE SAY?

HE DID ASK ME ABOUT SOME KIND OF DEVICE THAT SHOULD HAVE BEEN FOUND ON ME. DO YOU KNOW WHAT HE'S TALKING ABOUT, PETRUS?
WELL--

WHAT IS THIS DEVICE SUPPOSED TO DO?

IT BROUGHT ME HERE, I GUESS.
NICHOLAS, HE SAID I INVENTED IT.

THAT'S WHAT I WAS AFRAID OF.
EXCUSE ME, SIR?
MEN, TAKE HER INTO CUSTODY. THAT'S AN ORDER.
WAIT. WHAT'S GOING ON?!
RELAX, MS. HINDE. THIS IS FOR YOUR OWN GOOD.
PETRUS, WHAT THE HELL IS THIS? I'M ON YOUR SIDE HERE.
I'M SORRY JANE. PLEASE... JUST GO WITH THEM PEACEFULLY.
YOU SURE THIS IS THE RIGHT CALL?
IT'S THE ONLY CALL. THOSE CREATURES WILL DESTROY US ALL.
AND JANE, IT APPEARS, IS THE KEY TO STOPPING THEM.

Chapter 3

MAY I COME IN?

DO I HAVE A CHOICE?

I DIDN'T HAVE A CHOICE, TOO.
EVERYONE HAS A CHOICE. WHETHER OR NOT YOU KNOW IT IS A DIFFERENT STORY.

WE'VE BEEN WORKING *TOGETHER* FOR THREE YEARS.
AND NOW I'M UNDER HOUSE ARREST, TREATED LIKE SOME KIND OF HOSTILE WITNESS?
WHAT HAPPENED TO OUR *TRUST?*

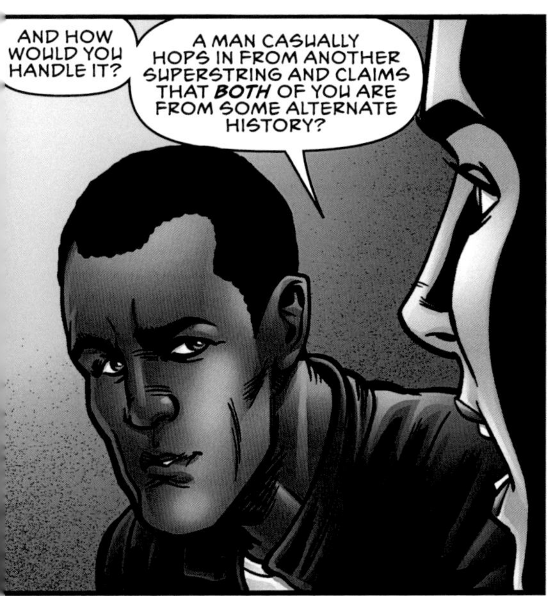
AND HOW WOULD YOU HANDLE IT?
A MAN CASUALLY HOPS IN FROM ANOTHER SUPERSTRING AND CLAIMS THAT *BOTH* OF YOU ARE FROM SOME ALTERNATE HISTORY?

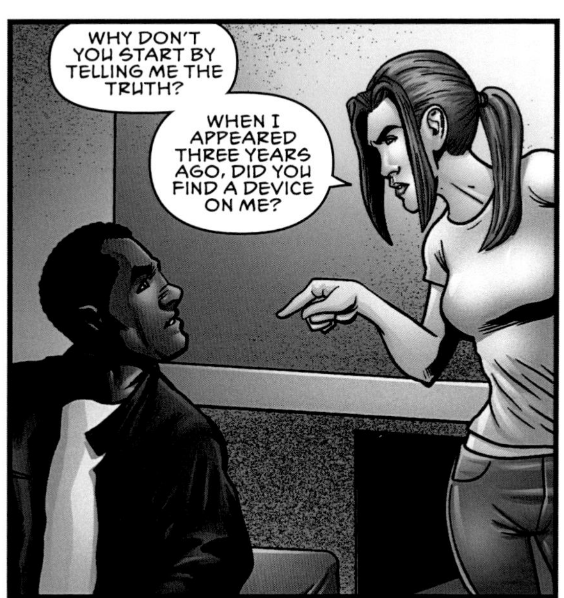
WHY DON'T YOU START BY TELLING ME THE TRUTH?
WHEN I APPEARED THREE YEARS AGO, DID YOU FIND A DEVICE ON ME?

YES.

PLEASE. SIT BACK DOWN. I HAVE SOMETHING TO SHOW YOU.

HOTEL ATTRACTION
GREENWICH STREET
YOU CAN'T GO IN THERE! *MIJNHEER* PATEK IS MEDITATING.
TRUST ME, HE'LL WANNA TAKE TIME OFF FROM NIRVANA FOR THIS.
AREN'T YOU DEAD, DR. ZACHARIAS?
OR AM I THINKING OF THIS WORLD'S ***VARIANT?*** YOU BOTH LOOK SO MUCH ALIKE.

LEAVE US, HE IS WELCOME.
YOU'RE HERE BECAUSE OF THE GIRL, I TRUST?
HER NAME'S ALEXA. AT LEAST, IT WAS. I NEED TO BRING HER HOME, BACK TO HER OWN COMPOSITION.
OUR *OWN* COMPOSITION.
IN MY STRING, YOU'RE A BRILLIANT SCIENTIST. FOUNDED ORINTECK. THE COMPANY THAT FUNDED US AND OUR RESEARCH.
AND YOU'RE HOPING I DID SOMETHING SIMILAR HERE.
I SEE YOUR MEDALLION HERE. I JUST NEED TO KNOW, ARE YOU WILLING TO HELP THE *CAUSE?*
PHINEAS. BE A DOLL AND GET US SOME TEA. DR. ZACHARIAS AND I ARE GOING TO BE A WHILE.

WE DON'T KNOW WHAT IT DOES, BUT WE SUSPECT THIS IS WHAT LET YOU JUMP BETWEEN COMPOSITIONS.
AND IT'S BEEN LOCKED UP IN THE VAULTS SINCE THAT DAY?
YOU HAVE TO UNDERSTAND, WHEN YOU FIRST APPEARED, NO ONE TRUSTED YOU. WE HAD NO IDEA WHO YOU WERE OR WHAT WE WERE DEALING WITH.
AND, WELL, NOTHING IS AS PERMANENT AS A TEMPORARY MEASURE.
SO WHY SHOW ME NOW?
THE VERSLINDER.
THEY FIRST STARTED APPEARING SIX MONTHS AGO.

THESE THINGS CAN'T BE KILLED. WE'VE TRIED. THEY'RE IN SOME SORT OF *TEMPORAL FLUX.*
ALL WE KNOW IS THAT THEY'RE DESTROYING THE FABRIC OF SPACE AND TIME AROUND THEM.
THEY'RE *DEVOURING* IT, QUITE LITERALLY.

SO YOU THINK THIS DEVICE, WHATEVER IT IS, MIGHT BE THE WAY TO STOP THEM.

MAYBE. IF WE KNEW ANYTHING ABOUT IT.
THERE'S ONE THING THEY DIDN'T TRY... DEEP BRAIN STIMULATION.
THE TROUBLE IS, I DON'T REMEMBER. WE'VE TRIED EVERYTHING.

NO. THAT'S CRAZY.
IF THERE WAS EVEN A SLIVER OF MY FORMER SELF IN THERE, IT WOULD'VE COME OUT BY NOW.

THEY MIGHT AS WELL KILL ME.
I'M SORRY, JANE. REALLY...

WELTERUSTEN, GOOD DOCTOR. WE'LL TALK SOON.
DO YOU THINK WE CAN TRUST HIM?
I DON'T KNOW. WE DON'T EVEN KNOW WHICH VARIANT WE'RE DEALING WITH HERE.
HE COULD BE FROM THE GIRL'S HOME-WORLD.
OR HE COULD BE LYING.
EITHER WAY, WE NEED TO CONNECT WITH OUR VARIANT BROTHER FROM THAT COMPOSITION.
WE LOST CONTACT WITH HIM SOME TIME AGO. HE COULD BE DEAD--
OR WORSE.

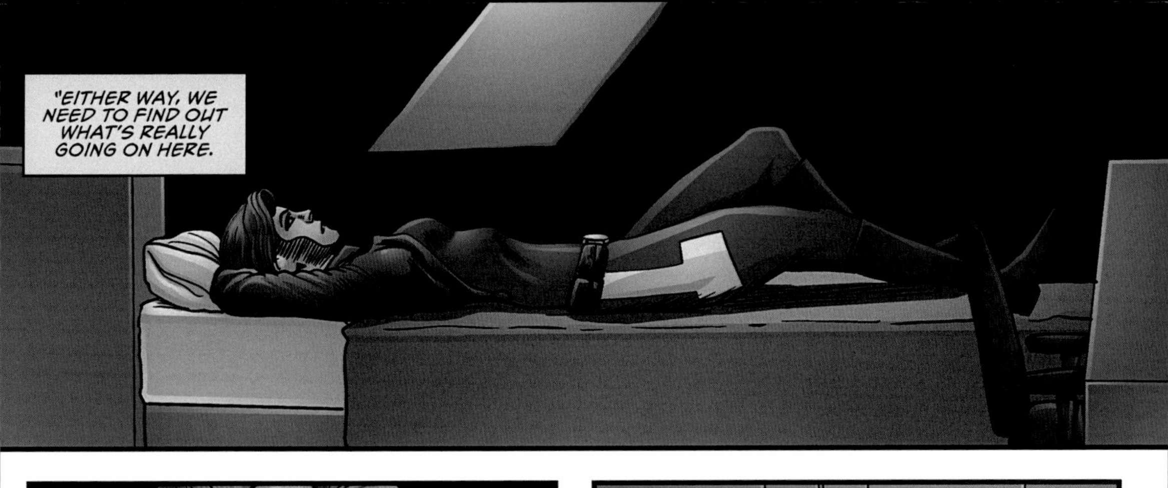
"EITHER WAY, WE NEED TO FIND OUT WHAT'S REALLY GOING ON HERE.

"WHAT IS NICHOLAS'S ENDGAME?

"AND WHY IS THIS GIRL SO DAMN IMPORTANT?"

Chapter 4

C'MON JANE. YOU CAN DO THIS.
INMAN

"THERE SHE IS...

...HEADING STRAIGHT FOR THE VAULT, AS EXPECTED.
I DON'T LIKE THIS.

WE COULD'VE JUST *GIVEN* IT TO HER.
WE DON'T KNOW HER. HELL, SHE DOESN'T EVEN *KNOW* HERSELF.
ARE YOU WILLING TO BET EVERYTHING WE HAVE ON *THAT?*
THAT'S WHAT I THOUGHT. NOW...
DID YOU MANAGE TO PLANT THE TRACKING DEVICE ON HER?
OF COURSE.
"DON'T WORRY, PETRUS... I'M SURE SHE WOULD APPROVE OF WHAT YOU'RE DOING.
BINGO.
"AFTER ALL, IT'S FOR THE GREATER GOOD.
"YOURS AND HERS."

HUH. SO I INVENTED THIS?
SCREEEEEE
CRAP.
AND TRIPLE CRAP.

SCREEEEEEEEEF
VERSLINDER!
WHAT THE HELL ARE THEY DOING?!
THEY'RE MULTIPLYING.
AT THIS RATE, THE ENTIRE BUILDING WILL BE OVERRUN IN A FEW MINUTES.

DAMMIT. I'M DETONATING THE BUILDING. IT'S THE ONLY WAY TO SLOW THEM DOWN.

WHERE THE HELL ARE YOU GOING?
WHERE DO YOU THINK?
CLIK

YOU HAVE FIVE MINUTES!

SCREEEEEEEEEEE
RATATAT TATTAT

!

SHHH... I'M HERE TO HELP.

WHO ARE YOU?
DR. VICTORIA CHEN...
I KNOW, I KNOW. THAT'S MY REAL NAME. THE PERSON I'M *POSSESSING?* I THINK HE'S CALLED KEVIN INMAN. I'M NOT REALLY SURE.
GEEZ, IT'S SO WEIRD HAVING A BEARD. AND I THOUGHT HAIR UNDER MY ARMS WAS ANNOYING.
ANYWAY, YOU'RE PROBABLY REALLY CONFUSED RIGHT NOW, AREN'T YOU?
YEAH.
SORRY, DOCTOR. YOU SEE, I'M YOUR ASSISTANT, AT LEAST I WAS BACK IN THE *OTHER* SUPERSTRING. AS YOU CAN GUESS, I'M A LITTLE NERVOUS. THIS IS MY FIRST *JAUNT* IN SOMEONE ELSE'S SKIN...
GOT IT. YOU'RE JUST POSSESSING THIS... KEVIN.

IN A SENSE. MIND TRAVEL WAS THE FIRST AND EASIEST WAY FOR US TO TRAVERSE SUPERSTRINGS. WHICH YOU HELPED DISCOVER. BUT DR. ZACHARIAS PROBABLY TOLD YOU ALL THIS AND--
JUST CUT TO IT. WHERE IS HE?

SEE? JUST AS SHARP AS EVER. FOLLOW ME. I'M HERE TO HELP GET YOU TO THE GOOD DOCTOR. HE'S WAITING FOR YOU.

WE'VE BEEN WATCHING YOU FOR MONTHS BEFORE DR. Z ATTEMPTED TO MAKE CONTACT.
SO WHAT'S THE PLAN? WHAT CAN NICHOLAS DO TO GET MY MEMORY BACK THAT THE PROTECTORAAT CAN'T?
THERE ARE SEVERAL PROTOCOLS WE CAN TRY. I'M NOT SURE WHICH HE HAS IN MIND.
EMERGENCY EXIT ONLY.
SECURITY CLEARANCE DELTA REQUIRED.
MAYBE THE *SUSSKIND TECHNIQUE?*
BUT IT'S NOT DEEP BRAIN STIMULATION, RIGHT?
NO. OF COURSE NOT. THAT'S SO... *INVASIVE.*
JUST CHECKING.
WHOOSH
HE'S WAITING FOR YOU AT THE TOP OF THE *HOTEL ATTRACTION.*
GREAT. THANKS FOR YOUR--
JANE!
SCREEEEEEEEE
RATATATAT
EDUARDO?

NO!
WHAT ARE YOU DOING? YOU HAVE TO ESCAPE! I'M ABOUT TO LOSE CONTROL OF THIS BODY.
I CAN'T HOLD THIS EXIT OPEN FOR MUCH LONGER. YOU'LL BE ON YOUR OWN.
I ALREADY AM.
PETRUS! HEADS UP!
YOU SHOULDN'T HAVE COME BACK. THE BUILDING... WE WIRED IT TO BLOW!
AND LET YOU HOLD IT OVER ME LATER? NO THANKS.

ALMOST THERE!
GOT IT!
GO. JUST GO.
NO. IT CAN'T END THIS WAY. IT *CAN'T*.

Chapter 5

WHAT THE--
FOOOOM
SCHOOOM

IT'S *GONE.* THE WHOLE THING...LIKE IT WAS NEVER HERE.
THE VERSLINDER... THEY DID THIS.

THIS IS JUST THE BEGINNING. THESE CREATURES ARE SPREADING.
CREATURE. SINGULAR.
THEY WERE ALL IDENTICAL. LIKE THEY WERE *CLONES* OR SOMETHING.
HOLD STILL. LET ME TAKE A LOOK.
I DON'T REMEMBER GETTNG OUT OF THERE. MUST'VE BLACKED OUT.
WELL? WHAT'S THE DAMAGE?
I DON'T KNOW. I'VE NEVER SEEN ANYTHING LIKE IT.
BUT I KNOW SOMEONE WHO MIGHT.

HOTEL ATTRACTION
STILL TRUSTING THE ENEMY I SEE?
HE'S HURT, NICHOLAS. WILL YOU HELP ME OR NOT?
ACTUALLY, HE'S DYING. THOSE BLACK LINES ON HIM ARE THE MARK OF THE VERSLINDER.
YOU REALIZE THIS MAN IS THE REASON YOU WERE LOCKED UP IN THE FIRST PLACE?
I'M ALSO THE REASON SHE ESCAPED.
LOOK, I GOT THE DEVICE, JUST LIKE YOU WANTED. HELP ME SAVE HIM AND IT'S YOURS.
THAT'S NICE. EXCEPT THAT I CAN'T USE IT. ONLY YOU CAN.
THE DEVICE OPERATES ON A NEURAL KEY -- A COMBINATION OF BRAIN PATTERNS ONLY YOU CAN CREATE.
AND HOW EXACTLY DO I DO THAT?
THAT'S WHERE I COME IN.

ORIN PANEK? YOU'RE THE *RICHEST* MAN IN THE WORLD. IS THIS...YOUR PLACE?
ACTUALLY, I OWN THE WHOLE BLOCK...I DON'T BELIEVE IN THE CONCEPT OF NEIGHBORS.
AND DON'T WORRY ABOUT THE PROTECTORAAT BOTHERING US THIS TIME.
I OWN THEM TOO. MORE OR LESS.
THIS IS THE SAME DRUG YOUR FRIEND DOCTOR CHEN USED TO JAUNT BETWEEN WORLD LINES.
PHYSICALLY, YOU'LL REMAIN HERE BUT YOUR MIND WILL WANDER BETWEEN ADJACENT SUPERSTRINGS. WE BELIEVE IT WILL RESTORE YOUR MEMORIES.
JAUNT? THAT'S CUTE A TERM. SHOULD I PACK A PICNIC BASKET?

I APPRECIATE YOUR HUMOR, BUT THIS IS SERIOUS. THE VERSLINDER CAN AND WILL COMPLETELY DESTROY THE FABRIC OF SPACE AND TIME HERE.
WE NEED THAT DEVICE TO WORK IF WE'RE GOING TO GET OUT OF HERE.

THEN YOU CAN TAKE IT YOURSELF. BECAUSE I'M NOT RUNNING.

YOU WANT US TO JUST ABANDON THIS WORLD? I THOUGHT YOU CLAIMED TO BE MY HUSBAND.
CAUSE IF YOU WERE, YOU'D KNOW I DON'T *ABANDON* PEOPLE. NOT WHEN I HAVE A CHANCE TO HELP THEM.
HAHAHAH!
YOU HAD ME, ALEXA. YOU REALLY DID.
WHAT THE HELL IS SO FUNNY?
YOU'VE CHANGED. NOT FOR THE BAD. BUT...YOU'RE DIFFERENT.
UNFORTUNATELY, THERE IS NO STOPPING THE VERSLINDER. YOU CAN'T KILL THEM. YOU CAN'T FREEZE THEM.
YOU CAN ONLY SLOW THEM DOWN.

IF WE'RE LUCKY, THEY'LL TRAP THEMSELVES IN THIS SUPERSTRING AS IT COLLAPSES ON ITSELF.
SO THAT'S IT THEN?
I'LL TELL YOU THIS MUCH, IF THERE IS A CHANCE TO STOP THEM? IF YOU *COULD* BE A HERO?
DISCOVERING WHO YOU WERE IS OUR ONLY OPTION.

UNGH!
PETRUS... STAY WITH ME!
I HAVE SOMETHING THAT CAN STABILIZE HIM.
PERHAPS IF YOU DO FIND A WAY TO STOP THE VERSLINDER YOU CAN SAVE HIM TOO?
NNNNGG.
FINE. GIVE ME THE DRUG. LET'S GET MY MEMORIES BACK.
WE ALREADY DID.

YOU'RE FEELING THE DRUG'S EFFECTS. IT ALTERS YOUR PERCEPTION OF TIME.
TRY TO RELAX. LET YOUR MIND DRIFT. WHAT YOU'RE FEELING IS NORMAL.
TO ME YOU'LL ALWAYS BE ALEXA.
YOU KNOW, FOR A THREE YEAR OLD, YOU HAVE A LOT OF ANXIETY, MS. HINDE.
"I'M JUST NERVOUS. WE'VE NEVER BEEN SO CLOSE TO FINDING OUT WHERE I CAME FROM."

Chapter 6

WHO AM I?
WHO WAS I?
I DON'T WANT MY PAST TO DEFINE ME. BUT WITHOUT IT, HOW CAN I KNOW WHY I'M HERE... WHO NICHOLAS IS...
OR HOW TO STOP THE VERSLINDER?

NEW YORK, 2019

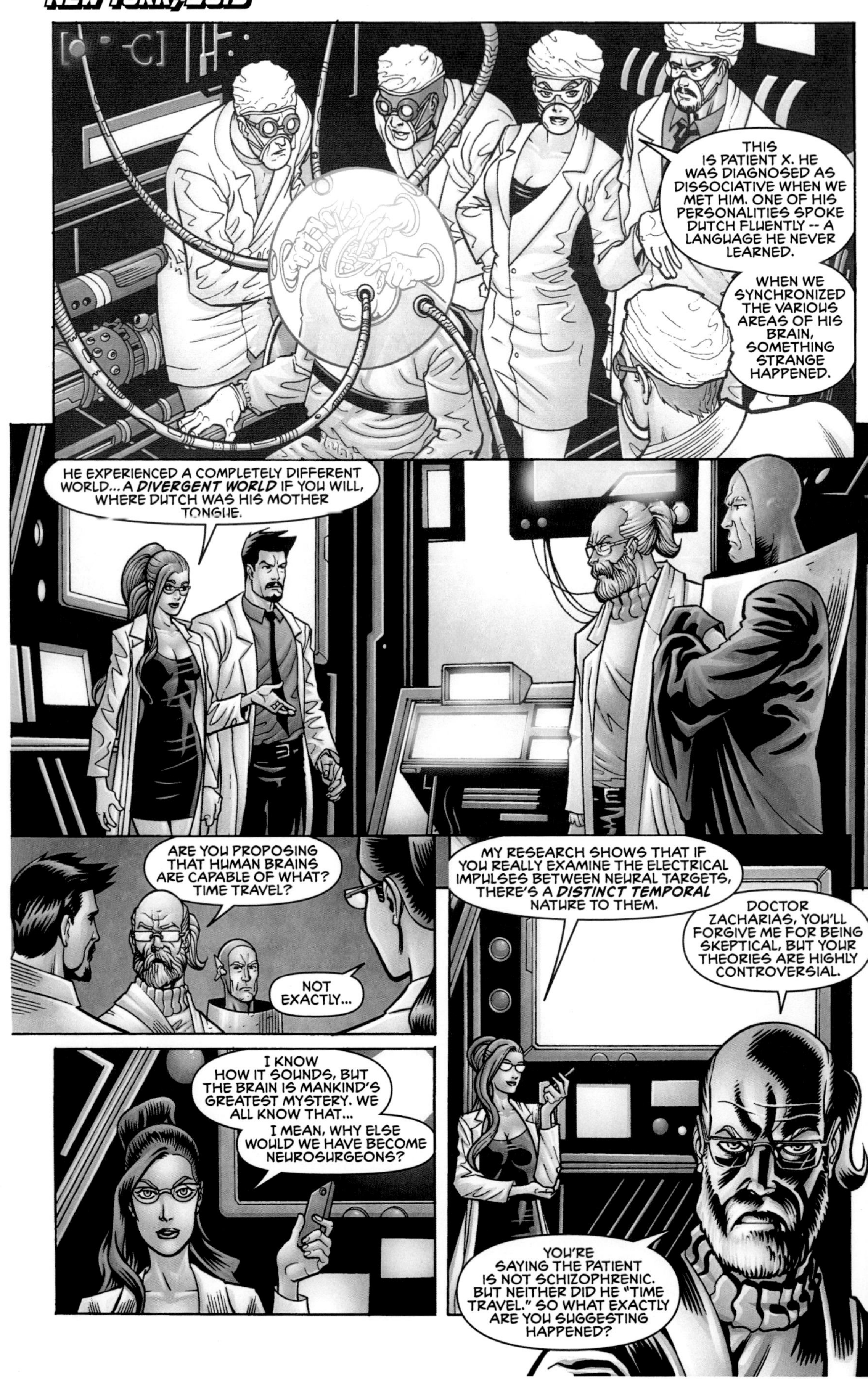

THAT WAS A TRAIN WRECK. DID YOU SEE THE WAY THEY LOOKED AT US?
YOU WERE GREAT, HONEY. DON'T BEAT YOURSELF UP.
THESE GUYS WERE OUR LAST HOPE. IF WE DON'T GET THIS FUNDING...ALL OUR WORK IS FOR NOTHING.
OUR IDEAS ARE JUST AHEAD OF THEIR TIME.
IT'S NOT YOUR FAULT.
YOU DO KNOW THEY'RE PROBABLY IN THERE LAUGHING AT US? JUST LIKE EVERYONE BACK IN SCHOOL.
AM I INTERRUPTING SOMETHING?
NO, NOT AT ALL. WE WERE JUST... WE...
JUST GIVE IT TO US, DR. PANEK.
THE BOARD SAID NO.
BUT THIS IS MY COMPANY AND I SAID, "YES."
WELCOME TO ORINTEK.

IT WAS AMAZING, NICHOLAS. THEY DON'T CALL IT NEW YORK... IT'S *NIEUW ORANGE.*
I THINK THAT'S HOW YOU PRONOUNCE IT, AT LEAST.
THEY BROKE OFF FROM OUR WORLD LINE IN 1673 WHEN THE DUTCH RETOOK NIEUW AMSTERDAM, IT APPEARS. EVERYTHING CASCADED FROM THERE!
HEY.

DR. CALLAGHAN!
I'M GUESSING YOUR JAUNT WAS A SUCCESS.
RESOUNDINGLY. THE NEW COCKTAIL GAVE US A MUCH LONGER WINDOW IN THEIR WORLD LINE. ALEXA MANAGED TO LATCH ONTO A SUBJECT FOR THREE HOURS. A NEW RECORD.

I'M JUST SORRY WE COULDN'T DEVELOP THIS SOONER. POOR ORIN...HOW'S HE DOING?
HE'S STABLE. BUT IT'S DOUBTFUL HE'LL EVER COME OUT OF THE COMA.
NO MATTER WHAT DRUGS WE CREATE, THERE WILL ALWAYS BE UNINTENDED SIDE EFFECTS.

ACTUALLY, THERE MIGHT BE A WAY AROUND THE SIDE EFFECTS. *PERMANENTLY.*
I WANT TO SHOW YOU A PROTOTYPE I'VE BEEN WORKING ON.

WHAT IS IT?
THIS IS THE FUTURE OF HYPERCOSMIC JAUNTS. IT STIMULATES CEREBRAL TEMPORAL TARGETS THE SAME WAY THE DRUGS DO, THROUGH ELECTRICAL IMPULSES.
YOU PAIR IT WITH A CRANIAL IMPLANT MADE COMPLETELY OUT OF ORGANIC MATERIALS. WE'VE BEEN WORKING WITH THE NEUROMORPH GROUP FOR THAT.
AND YOU THINK THIS WILL OFFER A STABLE WAY FOR THE MIND TO JAUNT TO OTHER SUPERSTRINGS?
BETTER THAN THAT.
WE THINK IT WILL ALLOW FOR *CORPOREAL* TRAVEL. FORGET RIDING SHOTGUN IN SOMEONE ELSE'S BRAIN...
YOU CAN VISIT THESE WORLDS ***IN PERSON.***

CORPOREAL TRAVEL? IS THAT SAFE?
WE INTEND TO FIND OUT. ALLOW ME TO SHOW YOU THE EXOSUIT ONE.
WE DESIGNED IT TO AID IN OUR JAUNTS. IT'S ABLE TO WITHSTAND EVEN THE HARSHEST OF ENVIRONMENTS.
JUST IN CASE THE WORLD WE JUMP INTO ISN'T... HABITABLE.
HOW SOON BEFORE WE CAN START HUMAN TRIALS?

HOTEL ATTRACTION, 2023
SHE'S BEEN OUT SIX HOURS. WE CAN'T LEAVE HER UNDER MUCH LONGER.
HER MIND COULD HAVE WANDERED TO ANY OF THE TEN TIMELINE-COMPOSITIONS. IF WE LEAVE HER TOO LONG, SHE WON'T BE ABLE TO COME BACK.
SHE'LL MAKE IT. TRUST ME.
I HOPE YOU'RE RIGHT. BECAUSE WE DON'T HAVE MUCH TIME.
THE VERSLINDER WILL BE HERE SOON. HALF THE CITY IS ALREADY GONE.

MOST OF THESE ARE PROTOTYPES. TOO DANGEROUS TO PUT INTO PRODUCTION.
THIS IS A BAD IDEA. WE SHOULD GET OUT OF HERE.
IF WE MOVE ALEXA NOW HER MIND MIGHT NOT FIND ITS WAY BACK. IT COULD KILL HER.
SO COULD STAYING HERE.
CAUSE HERE THEY COME.
WHICH IS WHY WE HAVE TO SLOW THE VERSLINDER DOWN.
CHEER UP. YOU'VE SEEN WHAT I CAN DO.
I'VE ALSO SEEN WHAT THEY CAN DO.
WELL I HOPE YOU LEARNED A THING OR TWO FROM IT...

Chapter 7

HERE WE GO!
SCREEEEEEEEE
BAM BAM
BAM BAM BAM
BAM BAM BAM

NEW YORK, 2020
THE IMPLANT IS STABLE, NICHOLAS.
BUT THE CONTROLLER ISN'T. IT'S TOO DANGEROUS.
WE TOLD CALLAGHAN WE WERE READY FOR HUMAN TRIALS.
IT'S NOT LIKE WE CAN JUST TEST THE DAMN THING ON A MOUSE.
AND IF IT FAILS? THEN WHAT?
HOW MANY MORE PEOPLE NEED TO END UP IN COMAS?
PEOPLE DIE. IT'S A RISK.
YOU THINK LOUIS PASTEUR DIDN'T THINK ABOUT THAT WHEN HE INJECTED THAT CHILD WITH THE RABIES VACCINE?
THAT KID WAS GOING TO DIE EITHER WAY. THIS IS NOT THE SAME.
FINE. I'LL TEST IT ON MYSELF. I'VE BEEN A GREAT GUINEA PIG THUS FAR.
ALEXA, PLEASE DON'T BE RIDICULOUS. WE'VE ALREADY COME THIS FAR.
PHYSICALLY TRAVERSING SUPERSTRINGS IS ICING ON THE CAKE.
JUST GIVE IT MORE TIME. PLEASE.
FINE. WE'LL DO IT YOUR WAY.

TWO WEEKS LATER
WHY EXACTLY AM I WEARING THIS MONSTROUS SUIT AGAIN?
BECAUSE WE DON'T KNOW WHAT KIND OF ENVIRONMENT YOU'LL BE TRAVERSING INTO.
I'M SURPRISED YOUR HUSBAND IS OKAY WITH THIS.
MY RESEARCH. MY CALL. HE KNOWS THAT.

I SEE. YOU DIDN'T TELL HIM.
LET'S HOPE YOUR AMBITION PAYS OFF.

DR. HAWKING, LET'S GET THIS STARTED.
ROGER THAT.

SEE YOU ON THE OTHER SIDE!

AAAIIIIIEEEEEEEE!!!
FZZZZZ
SHUT IT OFF!! NOW!

I HEARD WHAT HAPPENED. IS HAWKING DEAD?
NO. HE'S NOT THAT LUCKY.

WE THINK HIS BODY IS IN SOME KIND OF TEMPORAL FLUX. I DON'T KNOW. HE'S NOT DEAD. HE'S JUST IN... *DAMNATION.*

WE NEED TO DESTROY IT ALL. THE RESEARCH. THE PROTOTYPES. EVERYTHING. IT'S TOO DANGEROUS.

ALEXA! NICHOLAS! WE NEED YOU. SOMETHING'S HAPPENING.
WHAT IS IT?
HAWKING. HE'S *MORPHED.* I DON'T KNOW HOW ELSE TO EXPLAIN IT...
EXCEPT THAT HE'S DESTROYING *EVERYTHING!*

MY GOD... WHAT THE HELL?!
ORINTEK LAB, 2020
WE NEED TO RESTRAIN HIM. SOMEONE CALL SECURITY!
TOO LATE!
NO. THIS IS... THIS IS MY FAULT....
I DID THIS TO HIM!
I DID THIS TO HIM!

THERE'S TOO MANY OF THEM! I CAN'T KEEP THEM BACK!
SHE HASN'T STIRRED! WE NEED MORE TIME!
IF YOU HAVE ANY TRICKS LEFT UP YOUR SLEEVE, NOW'S THE TIME TO DO IT.
I'VE ALREADY DONE EVERYTHING I COULD.
THEN I GUESS THIS IS IT.
SORRY JANE.

WHAT... WHAT'S GOING ON?
YOU TELL US.
AS SOON AS YOU STIRRED THEY JUST... STOPPED.
I THINK I KNOW WHY.

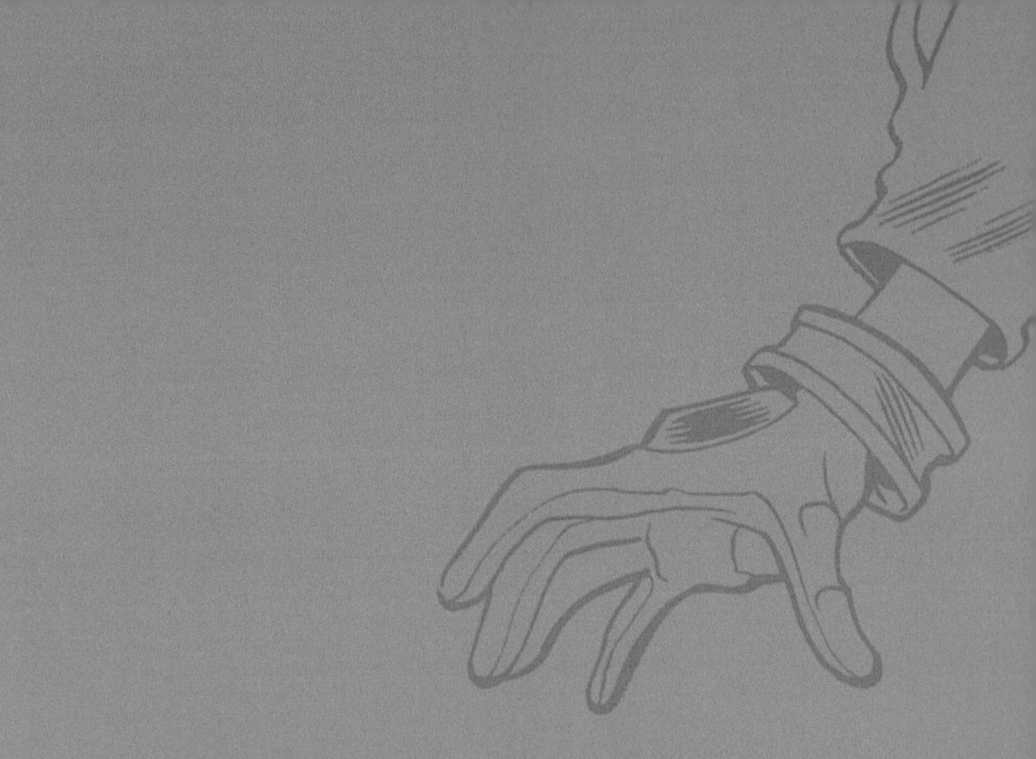

Chapter 8

WHY AREN'T THEY ATTACKING?
BECAUSE HE'S WAITING...
FOR ME.
ALL THIS TIME, WE THOUGHT THE VERSLINDER WERE CLONING THEMSELVES.
THEY'RE NOT. *HE'S* NOT.
WHAT DO YOU MEAN?
DR. HAWKING. ARE YOU IN THERE?
WHEN THE EXPERIMENT FAILED, IT PUT HIM IN TEMPORAL FLUX.
THESE AREN'T CLONES. THEY'RE ALL DR. HAWKING JUST... OUT OF PHASE.

THAT'S GREAT. BUT THAT DOESN'T CHANGE ANYTHING. THERE'S *NOTHING* WE CAN DO ABOUT IT.
AFTER YOU VANISHED, THE FIRST ONE REAPPEARED AND STARTED MULTIPLYING LIKE A PLAGUE. WE TRIED EVERYTHING TO DESTROY THEM.
HIM. HE'S A HIM.
IT.
DOESN'T.
MATTER.
OUR ONLY HOPE AT THIS POINT IS TO TRAP HIM HERE IN THIS STRING AS IT COLLAPSES. IT'S THE ONLY WAY.
AND IF HE FOLLOWS US AGAIN? THAT'S HOW HE GOT HERE.
NO. LETTING THIS REALITY COLLAPSE IS NOT THE ANSWER.

PLEASE ALEXA--
MY NAME IS JANE.
OKAY. I'M NOT WHOEVER YOU THINK I WAS. ALEXA IS GONE.

SO WHAT NOW, JANE?
THERE'S ONLY ONE THING I CAN DO.
USE THE DEVICE TO FIX THIS.

NOOOO!!

DR. HAWKING... CARL...
I'M SO SORRY.
I.... TRUSTED... YOU...
I KNOW. WHO I WAS... WHO I AM... THEY'RE TWO DIFFERENT PEOPLE. THAT DOESN'T FIX IT, STILL. BUT...
PLEASE. KILL ME. I CAN'T GO BACK TO BEING THAT... THING.

DO YOU EVER LOOK AT THE WORLD AROUND YOU AND THINK THAT IT ALL LOOKS WRONG?
AMAZING. SIMPLY AMAZING.
YOU DID IT, JANE. THEY'RE GONE. EVERYTHING'S BACK.
YOUR OWN POSSESSIONS. YOUR OWN REFLECTION. NOTHING IS FAMILIAR.
WHAT IF IT'S TRUE?
WHAT IF YOU DON'T BELONG IN THIS WORLD? AND YOU'RE NOT WHO YOU THINK YOU ARE?
MY NAME IS JANE HINDE. ONCE I WAS KNOWN AS DR. ALEXA ZACHARIAS. I INVENTED A DEVICE TO JUMP WORLD LINES.
AND IN THE PROCESS, I NEARLY DESTROYED EVERYTHING.
NOW I INTEND TO REPAIR THAT DAMAGE I CAUSED...NO MATTER WHAT THE COST.

YOU FAILED. THE HIVE WILL BE DISAPPOINTED.
I WAS ABOUT TO CALL YOU.
YOU ASSURED US THE VERSLINDER WOULD DESTROY THIS WORLD. THAT YOU WOULD RESTORE ALEXA TO HERSELF AND BRING HER BACK TO US.
AND I WILL.
I JUST NEED MORE TIME. SHE REMEMBERED MOST OF WHAT HAPPENED... BUT NOT EVERYTHING.
ONCE SHE DOES, SHE'LL HAVE NO CHOICE BUT TO HELP THE HIVE.
THE BEEKEEPER WILL GET WHAT HE WANTS.
AND MORE.
TO BE CONTINUED

The Origin of Nieuw Orange

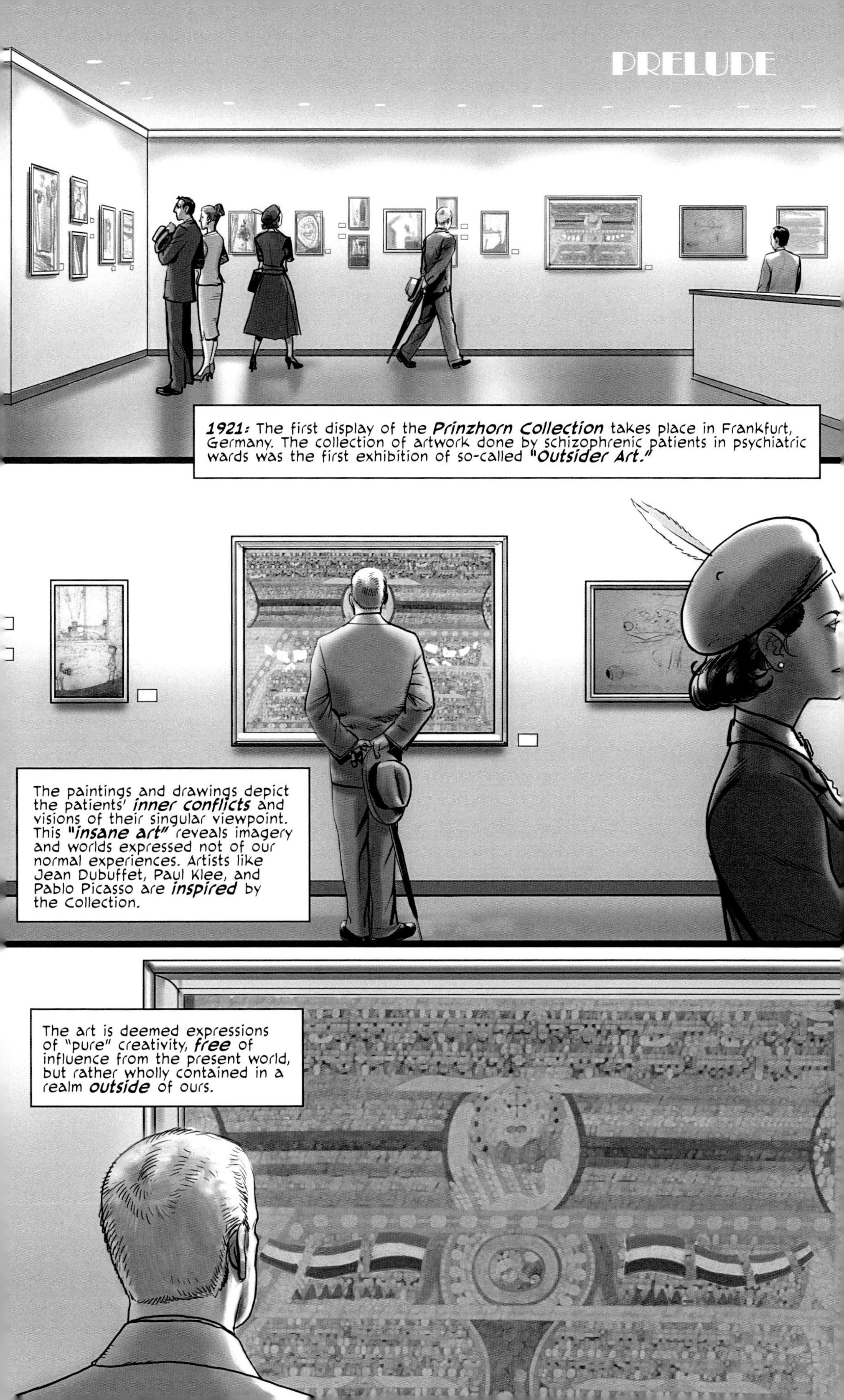
PRELUDE
1921: The first display of the Prinzhorn Collection takes place in Frankfurt, Germany. The collection of artwork done by schizophrenic patients in psychiatric wards was the first exhibition of so-called "Outsider Art."
The paintings and drawings depict the patients' inner conflicts and visions of their singular viewpoint. This "insane art" reveals imagery and worlds expressed not of our normal experiences. Artists like Jean Dubuffet, Paul Klee, and Pablo Picasso are inspired by the Collection.
The art is deemed expressions of "pure" creativity, free of influence from the present world, but rather wholly contained in a realm outside of ours.

Timeline
1673: Dutch Naval Captain Anthony Colve takes charge during the Third Anglo-Dutch war.
Nieuw Amsterdam is recaptured from the British and christened Nieuw Orange. The city becomes the European melting pot, pioneering the Dutch principles of tolerance and capitalism.
The combination of competition, diverse populations, and free trade shapes the character of the city, and of the region of Nieuw Nederland, which encompasses New York, New Jersey, Pennsylvania and Connecticut. New England extends from Rhode Island to Maine.
The Fort

1694: The delivery of £1 million to the Duke of Savoy. The HMS Sussex is not shipwrecked off Gibraltar.
This payment buys his loyalty and prevents his alliance with the French. This avoids a prolonged stalemate in North America and the French-English wars of the 18th century, which led to the American Revolution against the British Crown, which never occurs.
NIEU JARSEY
Lange Eyland
Matouwaes
Instead, a pragmatic treaty with the England, brokered by the Dutch, peacefully separates the colonies from the monarchy. The founding fathers still draft a Constitution and form a government with executive, legislative, and judicial branches.

1844: Henry Clay defeats James Polk in the presidential election. This rewrites the map of America. California is never acquired from Mexico.
Texas remains an independent republic, and the nation never expands westward into the continental United States. The American Federation will include Cascadia, extending from Oregon to British Columbia; the Central Lakeland Territory, Baja California, the Southern Confederacy, and the Greater Latin Principality.
Cascadia
Central Lake Territory
The American Federation
Baja California
Southern Confederacy
Texas
Greater Latin Principality
1874: Completion of the first phase of Alfred Ely Beach's Pneumatic Railway in Nieuw Orange.

1889: At a performance of Buffalo Bill's Wild West show in Berlin, Annie Oakley's attempt to shoot the cigar out of the mouth of Kaiser Wilhelm II goes wrong, and the Reich's most volatile leader is killed.
His successor does not pursue the same aggressive policies that led to Germany's protracted military campaign twenty-five years later.*
*David Clay Large, "Thanks, But No Cigar," What If? G.P. Putnam's Sons, New York, 1999. Edited by Robert Cowley. 290-1.
1907: Pablo Picasso exhibits Les Demoiselles of Avignon. It is the start of Cubism, as introduced by Picasso and George Braque. Henri Bergson described the movement as the "simultaneous combination of multiple perceptions and memories."

1909: Teddy Roosevelt's returns to Nieuw Orange as mayor after his presidency. Thanks to his progressive environmental policies, the oyster beds of the city remain fertile to the present day.
1910: Antonio Gaudi completes his Hotel Attraction on the World Trade Center site.
1912: RMS Titanic arrives in port in New York City.
1914: A young Adolf Hitler is gunned down by British troops in October with other members of the 16th Bavarian Reserve regiment at Gheluvelt.
1915: Germany wins an abbreviated WW1 after the Christmas armistice. With no German humiliation there would have been no National Socialism. There is no radical revolutionary movement in Russia called Bolshevism. No Russian revolution or Nazism means no World War II, no Holocaust, no purges, no gulags, and no Cold War. Lenin dies in exile in Switzerland.*
*Dennis E. Showalter, "The Armistice of Desperation," What If? 292-3.

1915: Physicist Ludwig Flamm
deduces the existence of wormholes.
1917: Nicola Tesla completes his experiments
in wireless power systems, plasma energy, and
antigravity airships. The Wardenclyffe Tower
experiment is a success.
1944: Britain lands
a man on the moon.

Present Day: The City of Nieuw Orange. Preserve Centraal South and 59th Street.
the Adjacent
written and created by Peter Zahos
concept art by John R. Holmes

About the Author

Peter **Zahos**

Peter Zahos is a neurosurgeon based in New York. He discovered the journals of Nicholas Zacharias within a delinquent reprint of the eleventh edition of the *Encyclopaedia Britannica*. This book was based on the first of several entries.